Extra-Extra! Read All About It!

"The response Erie Times-News In Education received when we published the serial story, *Julie & The Lost Fairy Tale* on our NIE *Extra-Extra! Read All About It!* literacy page was phenomenal. The story was an excellent choice to help us reach our goal of bridging the gap between the classroom and the real world.

It helped us foster communication with educators, students and their families and the entire community."

— Anna McCartney
Erie Times-News Newspaper in Education
and Literacy Projects Coordinator

"We eagerly anticipated the serialized stories. *Julie & The Lost Fairy Tale* was an especially good read, in addition to a fine vehicle for modeling 'showing writing.' The author's use of descriptive language was outstanding!"

— Pat Gustafson
Elementary Teacher in North East, PA

"The first chapters led to a great discussion about immigration. (This is significant because of the large number of immigrants that we have.) I particularly like the story because it is so well written."

— Cindy Munch
Elementary Teacher in Erie, PA

Fourth grade students of Cindy Munch at Pfeiffer Burleigh Elementary School in Erie, PA shared their thoughts about *Julie & Lost Fairy Tale.*

"When I read the story it makes me feel as if they (the characters) were here. I think it is a great story. READ IT!"

— Levina

"I like the Julie story. I wish it could go on and on forever! I think Julie is a brave girl and so is grandma. I think Mr. Malloy is a good guy. I liked the surprise ending."

— Paul

Julie & The Lost Fairy Tale was published in the *Erie Times-News* September through December 2004.

To Allyson, Adam + Amanda,

Dreams do come true—
Even if you have to wait
A very long time!

Julie
&
The Lost Fairy Tale

Julie
&
The Lost Fairy Tale

By

Janie Lancaster

Julie & The Lost Fairy Tale

ISBN: 1-932993-60-6
ISBN 13: 978-1-932993-60-8

Library of Congress Number
LCCN: 2006937731

Edited by Janet Elaine Smith
Front Cover Design by Cheyenne and Gwen Canfield
(lookingglass@canfieldfive.com)
Back Cover Design by Star Publish LLC
Interior Design by Mystique Design

A Star Publish Book
http://starpublish.com
Sun Valley, Nevada U.S.A.

Published in 2006 by Star Publish LLC
Printed in the United States of America

This book is dedicated to my grandmother,
Anna Horak.
Even though I only knew my grandmother for a short time,
my memory of her and of her loving-kindness to me will stay with me forever.

Acknowledgements

I'd like to thank all the people who were instrumental in bringing this book to life.

To Yvonne Nelson Perry, my teacher/editor, who worked tirelessly to help pull the story out from within my inward parts during our weekly critique group sessions and private talks.

To my sister, Susan Carol Howarth, who gave me the help and the courage to let go and send my story out into the world when it was first printed in *The Covington News* on September 2005 as a serial story.

To my friends who helped me with typing, editing and reading out loud. In alphabetical order:
Denise Anderson Nichols
Andrea Rosario
Swainee Rosario

To my innovative publisher, Kristie Leigh Maguire, who patiently helped me to get through the designing and finishing touches of this book.

And last but not least, to my loving husband Don who gave me the help and courage to hold onto and pursue my dreams.

Foreword

Fairy tale has many meanings in today's world. To me, fairy tale means a highly imaginative story that teaches a lesson or a story with a happily ever after ending.

History has recorded for the delight of us all so many of these highly imaginative stories—stories that have played a part in molding the lives of many of us to this very day.

Fairy tales taught me:

- It's ok to be an ugly duckling when you're small because one day you'll grow up to be a beautiful swan.
- You shouldn't cry wolf if there is no wolf around because when a real wolf comes, no one will listen to you.
- Don't be lazy if you build a house; build it strong so that no one will huff and puff and blow your house down.
- If we tell lies, every one will know because it will be as plain as the nose on our face.
- There's no place like home.

Mirror In The Attic

Chapter One
The Mysterious Travel Chest

I heard strange noises from the attic above me. I gripped the railing to climb the stairs and forced my feet to take the last few steps to enter my grandma's dusty old attic. The late afternoon rain pounded on the roof and the wind made a sound like howling dogs. My heart thumped and knees wobbled as a cold chill crawled up my back.

The floor creaked beneath me as I searched for a light switch, but couldn't find it. A beam of light flickered through the dusty oval attic window and revealed scattered discarded objects from the past. Spooky shadows danced throughout the room as cold winds slipped through cracks in the walls and made me shiver.

I was always curious about Grandma's attic in her old plantation-style home in Covington, Georgia, but never dared go up there. Darkness, spider webs and the musty smell kept me away—until now. Grandma said the noises we heard in the attic were probably coming from a mama squirrel making a nest for her babies. I had to see if there were baby squirrels hidden in the attic. Besides, a girl eleven years old shouldn't be afraid.

Using an old walking stick in a corner near the steps, I poked and pushed the sticky cobwebs out of the way. Old pictures, clothes, odds and ends were scattered about the room. I looked for the squirrels inside a toy wicker baby carriage and a wooden butter churn. Then I searched under a broken chair, a wobbly table and inside a box of chipped china cups and plates. Peeking underneath worn sheets and quilts, I found a big cracked mirror with a round wooden frame. Stacked behind the mirror were pictures of men in dark suits and women in long dresses. The women had their hair clamped tight in a bun with their lips pressed together. No baby squirrels to be found.

Then, in a dusty corner, I discovered a mysterious old travel chest. It was a wooden curved chest with ancient leather straps. It looked like a treasure chest. Were there secrets locked inside? Or maybe there could be a forgotten treasure waiting to be found. I tugged at the lock. The latch broke and fell to the floor. As I opened its creaking lid, I felt like I was about to discover a secret—a secret locked up for a very long time.

The musty smell from inside the travel chest made me think of old rotted bones, slithering things and crawly bugs. Shivers and goose bumps raced up and down my arms and legs. I quickly shut the lid. I wanted to run back down the long, winding stairs, but I had to know what was inside the travel chest. I forced myself to open the creaking lid again and peek inside.

I took a deep breath to calm my thumping heart. My eyes widened. I kept a careful watch out for creepy crawling things: roaches, spiders, or maybe even waiting rats.

Inside I found a floppy hat with a jacket and dress to match. There were worn-out black stockings, each one mended with tiny little stitches. I pulled out funny little bloomers with a string to tighten around the waist.

A child's travel chest. Yes. That is what it must be.

The clothes were just my size. I put on the hat and stood up. I held the dress up to me and spun round and round. The little girl who owned this travel chest must have been the same age as me. Were these Grandma's clothes when she was a little girl? Or did they belong to another little girl?

I looked at myself in the cracked mirror and imagined what it must have been like to live at a time so long ago.

Then I wondered what else was in the travel chest and began digging deeper beneath the clothes. There was a letter on top of a small stack of old, yellow, crinkled papers that were tied with string. It was in another language. Maybe it's written in German. I remember Grandma writing a letter to a friend who lived in Germany.

But this writing was a little different. Each word was written so carefully, kind of squiggly, as if it was written with an artist's quill. Did the little girl who wore this dress write the letter? Who was it written to? Was the letter never sent?

The stack of papers were written in the same language as the letter, but some of the shapes were different. What was written on this curious stack of papers? I thought about Grandma. Yes! My grandma, maybe she can read it to me. I'll take the letter and stack of papers to her.

I gathered the letter and papers that were tied up with string and set them on the floor, then refolded the clothes, put them back inside the small travel chest and closed the lid. Forgetting all about the noises and the squirrels, I took the curious written treasure down the long winding attic stairs to my grandma's room.

I hope it's written in German and I hope Grandma can read it.

Antebellum Home

Chapter Two
A Promise to Cordelia

I peeked into my grandma's bedroom. She was asleep. Poor Grandma still had the cold I had given her. Her nose was as red as a cherry tomato. Tissues piled up on the nightstand next to her bed could be lined up from her room to the backyard. I snuck into her room and put the letter and the stack of papers on a chair by the door. I sighed. I would have to wait.

I looked at the picture of my grandma on her dresser. In the picture, she was a little girl about the same age as me. My grandma was skinny with long curly brown hair and a freckled nose. I remembered what my grandpa used to say, "You and your grandma could be twins, except for your brown eyes and her blue eyes." Grandma would add, "Minus a hundred years." We would all laugh and laugh.

I loved this big old plantation home with its tall columns, high ceilings and carved wood. Most of all, I loved Grandma's bedroom with its poster bed, overstuffed green-striped chairs and fluffy flowered pillows. I liked to sit at the small table by the long windows and have tea parties with my grandma. But most of all, I loved this room, because it's my "Story Room" where Grandma reads stories to me.

Grandpa used to be here with us, pretending to listen, as he snored through most of the stories. I miss him and so does Grandma. I can't believe he died over a year ago.

The bed creaked and Grandma's eyes opened.

"Grams, you're awake? Are you feeling better?"

She blew her nose. "If I can keep my nose from falling off, I'll be okay."

"Oh, Grams, you're so funny even when you're sick."

"Well I don't feel funny," she said. "So what have you been doing while I was asleep?"

"I heard strange noises in the attic. I went up there to search for baby squirrels. Instead, I found a very old travel chest. These were inside." I picked up the stack of papers and took them to her. "I think they're written in German. And there's a letter to someone on the top of the papers."

I put the letter and stack of papers tied with string on Grandma's lap as she sat up in bed. After fluffing her pillows behind her, I snuggled in beside her.

"It's a letter," she said. Her eyes widened and her mouth dropped open as she read to herself. Then she stared off into space.

"Grams, what's wrong?"

"I'm sorry, Julie. Where did you say you found this letter?"

"In an old travel chest in the corner of the attic, under the oval window. Why?"

"That's Cordelia's travel chest," she said. "Why, it's been up there for fifty years. I forgot all about it."

"Fifty years? You mean you've had a time capsule in your attic all that time?"

"Imagine that." She tickled my ribs.

"Who's Cordelia?" I asked.

"She was my dear friend from a long, long time ago." Grandma sighed. "We were about your age when we met on a ship called the *Kaiser Wilhelm*. Cordelia was traveling from Germany with her mother and I was traveling from Austria with my older sister. We were on our way to Ellis Island in America to start a new life. We quickly became best friends—kindred spirits. Cordelia and I danced, sang songs and shared secrets with each other as we wandered around the creaky old ship."

"Where is Cordelia now?"

"When we arrived at Ellis Island, she didn't pass the medical examination and they sent her back to Germany. I'll never forget the look on her face when she gave me her travel chest to keep until she returned. She never did and I don't know whatever happened to her. I never heard from her again."

"Poor little Cordelia," I said. "What does she say in the letter?"

Grandma reached for her glasses and read the letter out loud.

Dear Editor:

My name is Cordelia Grimm, great, great, granddaughter of one of the Brothers Grimm. They were famous for fairy tales: Snow White, Cinderella, Hansel and Gretel, Rapunzel and so many more. Those were stories they gathered from around the countryside and put into books.

Fleeing from our home, I came upon a lost fairy tale that never made it into a book.

I am bringing this wonderful story to America to ask you to publish it for me.

Sincerely,
Cordelia Grimm

Grandma and I stared at the letter.

"Do you know what you found?" she said. "You found a lost fairy tale from the Brothers Grimm."

I shivered. "Oh, Grams, do you have them, too?"

"Have what, Julie?"

"Goose bumps." I showed her the blossomed little red bumps on my arms.

She held up her arm as we looked.

"No goose bumps on yours." I shook my head.

She put one hand over her heart and sighed. "Oh, but I have them here."

I put a hand over my heart and patted my chest. "Goose bumps in here too."

We both giggled.

Grandma untied the string around the stack of papers. "Well, let's read this lost fairy tale and see why it meant so much to Cordelia." She adjusted her glasses. She squinted and mumbled to herself as she turned the pages.

"What's wrong?" I asked.

"It's written in old German and much of the print is faded. I'm afraid I can't read it to you now, Julie. It's going to take time to figure this out."

"What? Wait? It's been lying in that old travel chest for fifty years and you're telling me I have to wait... You can't do that to me, Grams. Can't you at least tell me what it's about?"

"Julie, you have no patience. It has only been a short time since you found it—not fifty years. You can wait."

"Can't you just tell me an eensy-weensy bit?"

"Well, let's see, Miss Julie-No-Patience." Grandma sighed. Then she gave me a glance from the corner of her eye and scrunched her mouth to one side. She looked down at the stack of papers.

"The title is *Princess Momalina.* Let's see, what it's about. There's a small village and a little girl named

Katrianna Jonatina Breosio." She turned the page. "I think Princess Momalina is a doll, but I'm not sure." Grandma rubbed her eyes. "That's all. My eyes are tired. You'll have to be content for now, Julie. Let me rest."

I knew it was time for me to scoot. I got up off Grandma's bed and put both my hands over my heart.

"Katrianna Jonatina Breosio," I said as I waltzed out the door. "Don't you just love the way that name rolls off your tongue? Not like my name, Julie."

"Julie is a lovely name. I was there when your mother and father named you and it was beautiful to us," she said. "Now scoot."

Out the door I went.

In my bedroom that night, I made a promise to Cordelia. I promised her I would get *Princess Momalina* published. I didn't know how, but I would find a way.

Great Expectations
Printed In Newspapers First

Chapter Three
Julie Finds a Plan

The next morning I peeked in Grandma's room. She was sitting up in bed and writing in a small notebook. I skipped in and gave her a big hug. Her nose wasn't quite as red and her pile of tissues looked much smaller.

"Did you finish translating the fairy tale?"

"No, not yet," she said, squinting at me.

I sighed.

"What are you up to today, Julie?"

"I thought about taking our books back to the library." I walked over to the round table by the window and picked up Grandma's library books. I wanted to go to the library to find out about book publishers. I didn't want her to see my face. Grandma could always tell what I was thinking and I didn't want her to ask me a bunch of questions. I wanted to surprise her when I found someone to publish Cordelia's fairy tale.

"Good idea," she said. "I need some new books. I'll write the titles down for you before you go to the library. Why don't you go and get our breakfast?"

When I came back with tea, fruit cups and buttered scones, Grandma handed me a small notebook. "I have a little surprise for you. I translated the letter from

Cordelia and copied it into this notebook for you. When I finish translating the fairy tale, I'll write it in the notebook for you too. But for now, Julie, you'll have to be satisfied with the letter."

I put both my arms around Grandma's neck and planted a big kiss on her cheek.

I took the little notebook and was on my way to the library. I was glad that Grandma lived in a small town where everyone knew each other and she was sure they would keep an eye on me. I could go to town by myself.

I waved to some of the neighbors who were busy outside trimming bushes, painting fences and looking for mail in their mailboxes. Grandma was right. They kept an eye on me.

One time I complained to my grandma about the nosey neighbors. She told me the story about Mr. Hanson who lived alone in a small house down the street. He didn't like nosey neighbors, either. One day he got really sick and couldn't get out of bed. He would have died if it weren't for a nosey neighbor who noticed his mail piling up in his mailbox. Mabel Parker went inside his house and saved his life. Dr. Thomson said that one more day and he probably would have died. Mr. Hanson didn't complain about the nosey neighbors anymore. And I haven't complained about the nosey neighbors since.

Once I got to the library, I returned our books. Clutching the notebook in my hand, I walked up to the reference desk. Mrs. Peterson, the librarian, was sitting and organizing some file cards. Her gray hair was cut short around her gentle-looking face.

"Good morning, Julie," she said. "Need some help today?"

I knew I could trust her with my secret, so I showed her Cordelia's letter. I told her how I had found the letter and the lost fairy tale and now I wanted to find a way to publish the story and surprise my grandma.

She listened carefully and then she read Cordelia's letter. "Well, imagine that—a Grimm's fairy tale and Cordelia Grimm, a great, great, granddaughter to boot. I can't wait to see it get published."

My heart fluttered.

Mrs. Peterson smiled and motioned for me to sit next to her.

"There are many ways to get things published, Julie." She picked up a book on her desk, *Great Expectations,* by Charles Dickens. "Do you know where this book was first published?"

"No."

"It was published first in a newspaper and later into a book," she said. "Many writers got their start that way." Then she pointed to the display of magazines behind me. I turned around and looked at the pictures of ships, cakes, pies and even a Humpty Dumpty on the covers.

"There are magazines for everyone. And, that's just another way to get stories in print."

Mrs. Peterson got up and asked me to follow her to the back of the library.

"We also have many book publishers today," she said. "Let me show you where you can find them. There are shelves filled with books for writers." We walked down the long aisle. "Here's a good one." She pulled out a big book from one of the shelves and handed it to me. Then she went back to her desk.

I sat on the floor and opened the book. There were hundreds and hundreds of publishers. Maybe even a million. It was as if Mrs. Peterson had thrown me into the middle of the ocean and told me to swim to shore. I felt like I was lost at sea—a sea of never ending names and addresses. Finding the right publisher would be too hard and take so long. I can't do this.

I thought about taking the book to Grandma to have her help me, but changed my mind. She could not read such small print and then there would be no surprise if she helped me. Somehow, I will have to find another way.

On the way home, I walked through the park in the middle of town. I plopped myself onto a bench under a big oak tree. The sun was hot, but it felt cool in the shade. The clock on the town hall building across the street said it was almost noon, time for lunch. People were milling about and browsing in and out of the little shops across the street. Cars crept by, circling the park. I noticed a man sitting on a bench with a newspaper in his hand. He was reading an article to a boy next to him. They were both laughing.

That's my answer. I'll have the fairy tale printed in *The Daily Covington Times,* our town newspaper. Just like Charles Dickens. Then a publisher will read the story and want to publish the fairy tale into a beautiful book for children. There will be pictures of Princess Momalina, Katrianna and her village. That's what I'll do. But I won't tell Grandma just yet. I'll surprise her. First, I have to meet with the editor of *The Daily Covington Times.*

Cinderella Carriage

Chapter Four
Miss Eagle Eyes

Sparkling beams of light from a full moon lit up the town. I stood on the sidewalk and watched a creamy white horse pull a golden carriage shaped like a pumpkin around the town square. A woman sat inside. I tried to see her face but couldn't. A lacy white scarf about her head blocked my view. As the carriage passed by, I saw a license plate that read THE DAILY COVINGTON TIMES. Voices in the faceless crowd around me whispered Cordelia's name.

Banging pots and pans woke me up. I opened my eyes and sat up. The mysterious woman in the carriage was just a dream, but the noises in the kitchen were real. Grandma must be cooking breakfast.

I jumped out of bed. What will I wear? I'm going to meet the editor of the town newspaper today. My green dress was too short and my yellow flowered one made me look too young. I tried on my blue dress that had a collar with scalloped edges. It made me look older. This dress was the right one. But how was I going to explain to Grandma why I was all dressed up? She's used to seeing me in shorts and blouses.

As I walked down the stairs, I got an idea. I waltzed into the kitchen. "Today I am Katrianna Jonatina Breosio." I spun around and bowed. "How do I look?"

Grandma laughed. “Well, if it isn’t you, Katrianna. What a delightful surprise. Please, come and have breakfast with me.”

As she turned to pick up a pot from the stove, I sighed with relief and slipped into one of the wooden chairs at the kitchen table. My mouth watered as I watched my grandma dish out grits, scrambled eggs and bacon on our plates. “Yummy, Grams, I’m sure glad you’re feeling better.”

“Me too. Just don’t give me any more of your colds.” She shook her finger at me and we both laughed.

“Did you translate the fairy tale?” I asked after we finished eating.

“No, it’s going to be harder than I thought.” She got up to clear the table.

I slumped in my chair and rested my chin in my hands. How can I meet the editor of *The Daily Covington Times* without the fairy tale? I guess I’ll just have to show him Cordelia’s letter and explain about my grandma translating the fairy tale.

After I helped clean the kitchen, I took the notebook and went out the door.

When I got to town, I walked down Pace Street and then turned left onto Usher. As I stood across from the newspaper office, my knees trembled and my heart pounded. There was a big sign above the door of the stone building: THE DAILY COVINGTON TIMES. What was I thinking? I wanted to run the other way. Maybe this wasn’t such a good idea. I spun around toward home. Then I looked at the notebook and remembered my promise to Cordelia. She would be so happy to know the fairy tale was finally published. I took a deep breath, bit my lip, gripped the notebook and forced myself to walk across the street.

I squared my shoulders, opened the door and walked into the newspaper office. The desks in the entranceway were empty. At the end of the hall, two men were discussing an article on a page of the newspaper. Then they disappeared into a room. I tiptoed down the hallway and peeked into open doors. In one room, a woman sat at a desk typing. Piles of paper and newspapers were stacked up all around her. The bulletin boards on the walls were covered with notes. I wondered how she could get anything done in the midst of all that clutter.

A woman with jet-black hair slicked back in a bun suddenly appeared in front of me. She wore a starched white blouse buttoned tight at the neck and a long black skirt. Her eyes narrowed and her face looked rigid and pinched.

"What can I do for you?" she asked. She peered over her glasses at me with her eyebrows scrunched together.

"M—my name is Julie Sullivan and I—I'm here to see the editor," I said. I swallowed hard and felt my stomach tighten into a knot.

She motioned for me to follow her and then she looked in a big black book. "I don't have a Miss Sullivan down for an appointment to see Mr. Malloy," she snapped as she glared down at me.

"An appointment? Well, I guess I didn't..." My body stiffened. I forced myself to speak slowly. "I would like to make an appointment, if you please."

"You'll have to have an adult make an appointment with you. Children are not allowed to make appointments," she said, looking straight in my eyes.

"I am not a child," I returned her stare. "I am eleven years old and I'm here on very important business."

"Well, young lady, you will have to take your very important business somewhere else. The editor is a very busy man." She clamped her hands on my shoulders and ushered me toward the front door. She opened it and pointed a long, bony finger. I knew what that meant—OUT!

I pressed my lips together, clutched my notebook and marched out the door. My face felt hot and angry tears began to flow. How could she be so mean? My promise to Cordelia, how can I keep it now? I looked back and saw that woman standing in the doorway with her eagle eyes on me.

I stood against the outside wall of the newspaper office. Drying my tears with the collar of my dress, I tried to think of what to do next. I could never get past that woman. Not Miss Eagle Eyes.

Two men walked by me. One man headed toward the newspaper office, the other man away from it.

I heard the editor's name.

"Mr. Malloy, are you going to the park to eat your lunch?"

"Can't stay inside on a beautiful day." He pointed to the deep blue sky and puffy white clouds. "Besides, the squirrels in the park wouldn't be quite so fat if it weren't for me feeding them." He chuckled as he patted his round belly and showed the man a little brown bag.

My heart raced as I followed Mr. Malloy down the street. I ducked behind a woman pushing a baby carriage as I made my way to the park.

Mr. Malloy sat on a bench under a giant magnolia tree that was full of creamy white flowers. I stood across from him under the shade of an old oak tree. I watched him unwrap a big overstuffed sandwich and take a bite. His bushy eyebrows and the mustache on his pudgy face wiggled as he chewed.

This was my chance to meet the editor of *The Daily Covington Times,* but I couldn't move. I didn't know what to say. Would he listen to me? Does he really not like or talk to children? Will he think I'm just a little girl and send me away?

Mr. Malloy's Friend

Chapter Five
The Editor and the Squirrel

Mr. Malloy ate the last bite of his sandwich, got up and brushed the crumbs off his pants. My heart thumped. I thought he was going to leave. Instead, he opened a little brown bag and sprinkled some peanuts on the ground. A gray chubby squirrel with round-tipped ears and a bushy tail scampered down the tree and began to eat the peanuts. It sat on its hind legs and the tail curled like an umbrella over its head. Front paws held the peanut like a corn on the cob. The squirrel nibbled on the shell as pieces flew about. Tiny ears perked up and black-marble eyes widened when it got the reward of the two little peanuts inside.

Mr. Malloy put a peanut in the palm of his hand, bent over and offered it to the squirrel. He shook the peanut around in his palm and made a kissing, smacking noise with his lips. He scared the squirrel away. It ran up and down a nearby tree. It stopped and looked at Mr. Malloy and made clicking sounds. I giggled and walked over to show him what to do.

"It will never come to you that way," I told him. "Watch me. I come here to feed the squirrels all the time. I love squirrels. My grandma taught me how to get them to eat out of my hand. Here...give me your bag of peanuts and I'll show you how to feed the squirrel."

He gave me a doubtful glance as he handed me the bag of peanuts.

I took a handful of peanuts and placed each one on the ground in a row, about an arms-length apart. I sat down at the end of the row and held out the tip of the last peanut with my thumb and index finger. Without moving or making a sound, I watched the squirrel eat each peanut. It crept closer and closer to me. I looked the squirrel straight in the eyes and it looked right back at me. The squirrel jumped, grabbed the peanut out of my hand and ran up the tree.

"You did it!" Mr. Malloy said. "Not bad for a young whippersnapper. But I'm not sure I can get myself all tangled into the cross-legged position." We chuckled as he sat down on the park bench. "So tell me, do you live around here? And do you have a name?"

"Julie. I live in Morganton, North Carolina. I'm visiting my grandma for the summer. Her name is Mrs. Anna Bradshaw. She lives on Dogwood Lane."

His eyes opened wide. "Well, well," he said. His lips crinkled into a slight smile.

Then I remembered my promise to Cordelia.

I picked up the notebook. I stood in front of him and looked him in his eyes.

"Mr. Malloy, I have to confess something to you. I followed you here today. I tried to visit you at your office but..." I took a deep breath. "The woman who guards your office sent me away. I wanted to meet you. I have a very important promise to keep and I need your help." I handed him the book and showed him Cordelia's letter.

When he finished reading the letter, I explained how my grandma and Cordelia had met on the ship, the *Kaiser Wilhelm.* I told him how I found the letter and the lost fairy tale in Grandma's attic and that

Grandma had translated the letter and was now working on translating the fairy tale.

Mr. Malloy didn't say anything. He squinted and made little twists in his mustache while he listened to me.

I swallowed a big lump in my throat and continued.

"I went to the library to find out how to get the fairy tale published. I asked the librarian, Mrs. Peterson, for help. She told me about Charles Dickens, and how his stories were printed in newspapers first and then later into books. I thought about our town newspaper and that is why I wanted to meet you. To ask you to publish the fairy tale."

"Hmm." He put his hand under his chin, tilted his head to one side and looked at the letter again. "A Grimm's fairy tale," he mumbled. "And Cordelia Grimm, a great, great granddaughter of a Grimm brother."

I sat down next to him on the bench and looked at his face.

"It's a wonderful story," I said. "Grandma told me it's about a doll named Princess Momalina and a little girl called Katrianna Jonatina Breosio. Don't you think they are the most loveliest of names?"

"Interesting indeed. And you say your grandma is in the process of translating the fairy tale?"

"Oh, yes! And it shouldn't take her very long. She is very smart and she can read and write both in English and German."

"So you want to print it in the town's newspaper, do you?"

"Yes I do. You see it has been in that travel chest for such a very long time. And getting the lost fairy tale published was so important to Cordelia."

He jumped up, looked at his watch and handed me the notebook.

"Oh, I'm out of time," he said. "I'll let you know." He turned to leave. "Deadlines, you know, deadlines."

I stood there for a moment with my mouth hanging open as I watched him cross the street. Then I shouted, "But how? When? Where?"

It was too late. He was out of sight.

Julie Is Surprised

Chapter Six
Grandma Has a Visitor

The next day I went to the park to look for Mr. Malloy. He was nowhere to be found. I watched a squirrel scamper around me. It was the same fat squirrel with the round-tipped ears and big bushy tail that we fed yesterday. I sat slumped over on a park bench and sighed. The squirrel looked up at me. It sat on its hind legs with its little front paws wiggling in the air, begging me for a treat.

"I guess Mr. Malloy is not going to come," I said to the squirrel. "He's forgotten all about you and me. You'll have to find something else to eat and I'll have to find another way to publish the fairy tale story."

I hadn't told my grandma about meeting with Mr. Malloy. I wanted to surprise her. But there wasn't going to be a surprise. I got up and walked around the park one more time looking for Mr. Malloy. Then I trudged home toward Grandma's house. It was time to ask Grandma for help.

Maybe Mr. Malloy talked to Miss Eagle Eyes, I thought as I kicked a stone all the way home. No one ever listens to a little girl.

When I opened the front door, I gasped. I couldn't believe what I saw. Grandma was sitting in the living room with Mr. Malloy drinking tea and eating cookies. They were laughing together as if they were best friends.

"Mr. Malloy...you're here." I blurted out. "Grams, what's going on?"

I plopped into the big flowered chair in the corner and stared at them.

Mr. Malloy got up from his chair.

"You are going to have to explain it to her, Anna." He grabbed a big oatmeal cookie and headed for the door. "Deadlines, you know, deadlines." He smiled at my grandma, gave me a wink and said, "Julie, watch out for your grandma's dancing feet."

I sat and stared at Grandma. She looked at me, raised her brows and cocked her head to one side.

"So I'm smart, am I? Shouldn't take me a long time to translate the fairy tale, huh?"

I slumped deeper into the chair and forced a slight smile.

Grandma came at me with monster claws and tickled my ribs until we were both out of breath from laughing. Then she sat down on the couch and motioned me to come and sit next to her.

"You are an impulsive one and get me into trouble all the time," she said. "Just the same, I'm proud of you. It's quite imaginative and brave of you to get the fairy tale published on your own."

"Published? Does that mean he'll do it? Oh, Grams, I want to know everything." I turned my head and looked at her from the corner of my eyes. "And don't forget the part about the dancing feet."

She smiled, put her arm around me and tapped my nose. "Well, aren't you a nosey one. I guess you'll give me no peace until I tell you everything." She took a deep breath. "First, I'd better explain to you about Mr. Malloy and me. You see, Julie, Thomas and I went to school together a long time ago. We are old friends."

"And you and Mr. Malloy used to dance together?"

"Yes, we did. You'd never know it now. At one time, this little town had lots of parties. Many of them were in the park, in the middle of Covington Square."

"Were the two of you sweethearts?"

"No, just good friends. Let's get back to you, Julie. Mr. Malloy told me you went to his office and that his secretary ran you off."

"Yes she did. She is so mean."

"Mr. Malloy told me she could be a pickle sometimes." Grandma chuckled. "But you didn't give up, did you?"

"No."

"He also told me you followed him into the park and you taught him how to get a squirrel to eat out of his hand. Then he explained how you showed him Cordelia's letter and asked him to publish the lost fairy tale in his newspaper. When you told him you were my granddaughter, he decided to pay me a visit."

"So, he's going to do it? Publish the fairy tale?"

"How could he not want to? Mr. Malloy was quite impressed with your determination. Yes, he wants to print the letter and the fairy tale in *The Daily Covington Times*. He thought it would be a great human-interest story. To think, my clever little Julie, you did it through a squirrel."

"I did?" I jumped up from the couch and leapt into the air. "Oh, Grams, it's so wonderful. I can't wait to see it in print. When will he put it in the newspaper?"

"He didn't say when, only that he wants to."

Grandma got up, took me by the hand and danced me around and around the room. When we were out of breath, we fell into each other's arms in a humongous hug.

"Just imagine, Grams," I said, "Cordelia's letter and the Brothers Grimm's lost fairy tale, printed in *The Daily Covington Times*."

"Not so fast, Julie. It's not going to be that easy. Remember there's a slight problem of getting the fairy tale translated. It seems that a part of it is missing. I don't know. We are going to have to get help from experts to translate the fairy tale. "

"You mean it may take a very long time? Or it may not even get published?"

"Yes, that's a possibility, Julie. We'll have to wait and see."

Town Hall Clock Tower

Chapter Seven

A Buzz in Town

I searched the newspaper everyday but there was no letter—and no fairy tale. Then one morning when I was about to give up, my grandma's phone began to ring constantly. Grandma's friends were calling to talk to her about the letter from Cordelia Grimm that was published in *The Daily Covington Times*. They wanted to know if she knew anything about the lost fairy tale.

I ran outside to get the newspaper. It was nowhere to be found. I always laughed when my grandma searched for the newspaper that was carelessly thrown in our yard every morning. Today it wasn't funny. Where was it? I searched under bushes and around trees until I finally found it under the front steps. I grabbed it, ran inside and handed it to Grandma. She read the title on the front page: "*Covington's Hidden Treasure.*"

"What does it say?" I asked.

Grandma sat down at the kitchen table, spread out the newspaper and read it out loud.

It seems our little town of Covington is not only famous for its rich history and lovely antebellum homes.

A forgotten treasure has been found in the attic of one of our local residences. It is a fairy tale written by the Brothers Grimm in Old German. Now in the possession of The Daily Covington Times, *it is in the process of being translated. We will soon publish it for our readers.*

The fairy tale was brought into this country on a ship called the Kaiser Wilhelm *by Cordelia Grimm, the great, great granddaughter of one of the Grimm Brothers. On her way to America with the fairy tale, she was sent back home to Germany. She did not pass the physical examination due to a serious illness. She left her travel chest and the fairy tale with a trusted friend who kept it in her attic for almost fifty years. The name of the local resident and the finder of the treasure will be announced at a later date. At this time, we want to share with our readers a letter written by Cordelia Grimm. The letter was found in the travel chest along with the fairy tale.*

We looked at Cordelia's letter in the newspaper, then at each other and smiled. "Did you know Mr. Malloy was going to put Cordelia's letter in the newspaper today?" I asked.

Grandma winked at me and rolled her eyes. "Me, know a secret and not tell you?"

I put my hands on my hips. "You did know. Didn't you?"

"You're not the only one who likes to surprise people." The phone rang. "Saved by the bell," she said as she got up to answer it. It was another neighbor asking if she had read the article about the lost fairy tale. Grandma was careful not to tell anyone about the letter and fairy tale that I had found in her attic.

The buzz in town continued to grow each day. People gathered in the little park in the center of town and talked about Cordelia's letter, the fairy tale and days-of-old. I listened to the many stories they told about how their families ended up living in the town of Covington. Some came from nearby and others from far away. Covington became a town in 1822, but it was the railroad in 1840 that made it a thriving city. I learned the town was involved in the Civil War in 1860. The war split families and churches and caused great devastation in the area, but many of the beautiful plantation homes were left standing.

Day after day, the excitement grew until someone decided there should be a reunion. They would have an Extravaganza in the park and invite their families from far away to bring their old pictures and display them on family history boards. Invitations would be sent out and recipes from their homelands would be used to make food. Like old times, they would dance and sing in the park. It was to be an Extravaganza like nothing Covington had ever seen.

There were weeks of planning, writing letters, decorating and putting together history boards that would decorate the walls of the local firehouse recreation hall. People went to each other's homes to cut out pictures and paste them on family history boards. They talked about all their plans. Grandma's house was filled with people running in and out. An advertisement about the Extravaganza was placed in *The Daily Covington Times* and the news spread.

I helped Grandma with her family history board. We searched through all of her pictures and the things she had saved throughout the years. I went back and forth to the town library getting history books about Ellis Island and Austria, her homeland. It was fun to be part of this wonderful event.

"And to think this Extravaganza came about," Grandma said, "because of you finding the old wooden travel chest and feeding a hungry squirrel."

Mr. Malloy called and asked me to come to *The Daily Covington Times* the next morning. He said he had a surprise and not to tell Grandma that I was going to his office. I wanted to meet him in the park so I wouldn't have to run into Miss Eagle Eyes. He said I must come to his office, as he couldn't take the chance of being overheard by anyone.

I wondered what the surprise could be.

Newspaper Office

Chapter Eight
A Surprise

I stood across from the newspaper office. I didn't want to go in and face that woman at the front desk again. But Mr. Malloy said he had a surprise and I had to find out what it was. I took a deep breath, turned the doorknob and walked inside. Miss Eagle Eyes met me at the door and right away, I told her I had an appointment with Mr. Malloy. She quickly escorted me to Mr. Malloy's office. I couldn't believe it. I think she almost smiled.

Mr. Malloy sat behind a big mahogany desk. He leaned back in his chair. "I'm glad you came, Julie. Thank you, Miss Cragmeyer, I can take it from here." Miss Eagle Eyes left the room, shutting the door behind her.

I sat down in a wooden chair in front of Mr. Malloy.

He spoke to me in a soft, kind voice. "I have some good news and some bad news."

"Bad news?"

"Yes... We've had a great deal of trouble translating the fairy tale. Some of the pages were faded and hard to read. We had to call in an expert on the subject."

"Can they do it? Is it finished?" I leaned forward in my chair.

"No, not yet. It seems that the conclusion of the story is actually missing."

"Missing?"

"Yes." He put his hand under his chin. "The fairy tale ends with Katrianna and her family in flight and with the little doll, Princess Momalina, lost in the bushes. We can't publish a fairy tale with a sad ending like that, can we?"

"No, that would be like ending the story of Cinderella in tears because her step-sisters ruined her dress and she couldn't go to the Prince's Ball. So what are you going to do?"

"It's not what we're going to do; it's what we did. That's why I called you to come and see me—so I could tell you the good news. We found someone to translate the fairy tale. Maybe you should read this yourself." He opened a drawer, pulled out a letter and handed it to me.

I looked at Mr. Malloy and squinted. Then I began to read the letter.

My Dear Mr. Malloy,

I am looking forward to meeting you and visiting your town of Covington. I have almost finished translating the fairy tale. I'm afraid I will have to do the best I can with the lost ending. I could not read the last few pages, but I should be done with it by the time I'm ready to leave.

I am grateful to you for making my dream come true. I had forgotten about the fairy tale and my wish to get it published.

Please accept my gratefulness for the plane tickets that your newspaper sent me to come to America.

Tell Julie I shall arrive the day before the Extravaganza. We will have tea in my room and talk about how to surprise her grandma.

I am overwhelmed with excitement at the prospect of seeing my dear friend, Anna and her granddaughter, Julie. Best wishes.

Sincerely,
Cordelia Grimm

I stared at the letter with my mouth hanging open. Tears stung my eyes.

"Cordelia's alive and living in Germany? Grandma will be so happy. Oh, Mr. Malloy, I don't know what to say. It's the most wonderful surprise in the whole world."

"Now don't forget it's a secret."

"I know. It's a wonderful secret. And I promise I won't tell anyone."

I drifted toward home in a daze, thinking about Cordelia coming to America. When I got to the park, I thought about my dream of Cordelia riding in a golden carriage, circling the Town Square. I wondered what it would be like when she came to the Extravaganza. It would have to be a grand entrance for such an honored guest. I sat on a park bench and imagined different ways Cordelia could arrive at the Extravaganza. Maybe she'll come in a Cadillac convertible, a limousine or even a Rolls Royce. Then I imagined what she would look like—a queen with a crown, dressed in the finest silk and glittering jewels.

A woman pushed a carriage past me and I heard her baby cry. Startled, I glanced at my watch. Oh no, I'm late! Grandma told me she's making a special lunch. How I am going to explain? And how am I going to keep the secret about Cordelia from her? She always knows what I'm thinking and when I'm up to something. Grandma says I always give things away because I wiggle my body or roll my eyes. I'll have to be careful.

She met me at the door waving an accusing finger. "What's the excuse this time?"

I started to wiggle my body and roll my eyes. I clasped my hands behind my back and looked down at the floor. "Daydreaming... Grams, you know how I love to daydream."

"Yes, I do." She sighed. "Well, come and eat. I'm not going to hold it against you. I guess a child deserves to have dreams on her school vacation."

I sighed with relief and scooted off to the kitchen.

Grandma had gone to the farmer's market and bought fresh ears of corn and juicy red beefsteak tomatoes, my favorite summer food. She was silent through most of the meal. When we finished, I got up to help her with the dishes.

"Are you still mad at me for being late?" I asked.

"No, child. Why would you ever think that? You know I'm not one to hold a grudge."

"But you were so quiet while we ate our lunch."

"I'm sorry. I didn't realize it. I just feel a little down today. With all this talk about Cordelia and her letter, it's got me thinking. Maybe something awful happened to her. Perhaps she died on the way back to Germany."

I gulped. My face got hot and my body started to wiggle. I got myself busy clearing the rest of the table.

Grandma didn't notice my reaction. It was going to be harder than I thought to keep this secret from her.

Library Display

Chapter Nine

Family History Boards

The day before the Extravaganza, I went with Grandma to the firehouse recreation hall to put up our family history board. We saw other history boards already hanging on a wall. One of the firemen came over and helped us to hang ours. Seeing our family pictures and memories hanging on the firehouse wall made me feel so proud.

Grandma and I had searched through her pictures and letters involving her trip to America on the great ship, *Kaiser Wilhelm.* We had carefully taped the pictures, her boat tickets and all the letters on a big white piece of cardboard. We decorated it with ribbons and wrote names, dates and places under the pictures.

There was a picture of my grandma when she was eleven years old as she was getting off the ship. Her face was pale and her eyes opened wide. Around her head was a scarf and she had on a long dress. She looked so small standing next to her sister. The picture next to them was her uncle and aunt who had come down to the pier to meet them. Her uncle was tall with a serious face and a funny mustache with a downward twist on each end. Her aunt had on a bonnet and a full skirt with a buttoned jacket to match. She had dark eyes and stood rigid with her lips pressed tightly together.

Then I looked at a picture of Grandpa and me standing in front of the house. Grandma tapped me on the shoulder.

"Why the scrunched up face?" she asked.

"I was just missing Grandpa."

"I wish he could be here with us too, Julie." She put her arm around me. "Well, I'm sure tomorrow the Extravaganza will brighten up our moods a bit." She tightened her grip.

I looked up at her and smiled.

More people came into the firehouse. Sounds of laughter and loud voices echoed throughout the room. The long wall was filled with so much family history.

"Look, Grams." I pointed to one of the boards. "It's Mr. Malloy's family. I didn't know he was from Ireland and came through Ellis Island as a child."

"He did, and with all six of his brothers and sisters. They're scattered all over the United States. I think most of them will be here tomorrow for the Extravaganza."

"He must be so happy," I said. "I can't wait to see what they look like now. The boys look so cute with their little short pants, long socks and puffy round caps. And look at his father's big bushy mustache. Which one is Mr. Malloy?"

She pointed to a skinny boy with a bushy head of jet-black hair sticking out from under his cap.

I pointed to the picture and giggled. "It's hard to imagine Mr. Malloy ever having that much hair."

Grandma laughed. "Well, don't tell him that."

"Don't worry. I won't. I get myself in enough trouble as it is," I said. I motioned her over to the next group of family pictures. "Look, it's the woman who lives down the street, Maria Kovacs and her family. It says they came from Hungary. Look at their names. I don't even know how to say them."

"They're hard to pronounce," Grandma said. Then she pointed to each one. "Ilanka, I think, means Helen and this one is Aranka and Gyorgyi. Joska means Joseph. See the scarves the girls have on, Julie? They are called "babushkas." They were brightly colored with beautiful designs. The boy's caps were made from real animal fur."

"We dress so different now."

"Yes, we do. And we have stores to buy our clothes. Most of the clothes back then were sewn by hand," Grandma said.

"I'm glad we don't have to do that now."

We worked our way to the middle of the room where Mrs. Peterson, the librarian, had set up a display table in honor of Cordelia. She had pictures, books, essays and poems about *Ellis Island*. There was a picture of the *Titanic*, the *Kaiser Wilhelm* and other ships. The name, Ellis Island, was cut out of colored paper and pasted in the middle with photographs of buildings and the Statue of Liberty. We looked at the pictures of people sitting on benches, waiting in lines and wandering around Ellis Island.

I saw my grandma stare at one of the pictures of people waiting in a long line.

"What are you thinking, Grams?"

"I remember those lines," Grandma said. "We stood in line for doctors to examine us and then give their approval, only to be moved on to other lines, to wait and wait. Families and friends waited for us outside. They were praying we could pass through the many checkpoints so we could be reunited."

"The people standing in those lines look so lost and scared." I said.

She put her hand on my shoulder and smiled. "You see fear in their faces, Julie, but their hearts were filled with dreams and their heads filled with stories they had heard about America. They were a strong, determined people who had suffered a great deal before they came here. They were ready to do whatever it took to make America their home and build a new life."

"We're a part of that dream, aren't we?"

"You certainly are a part of mine," she said as she ruffled my hair and tweaked my nose.

I looked up at her and smiled. I put my arm through hers as we walked around and watched the Women's Club decorate for the Extravaganza. Streamers were draped throughout the room. Green tablecloths stretched out on long tables with candles and flowers. Balloons were taped in brightly colored clumps all around the room.

There was so much excitement in the air and so many visitors to our little town.

Later as Grandma and I walked home, we met Mrs. Annie Sullivan and her sister. Her sister had come all the way from Mississippi to visit Annie and attend the Extravaganza. They talked about their family history board and how much fun it was remembering and reminiscing about the days of long ago.

I whispered to my grandma after we crossed the street, "Her sister is so sweet and so very, very wrinkled. She must be very, very old."

Grandma laughed. "Don't be fooled by what you see on the outside, Julie. No matter how old we are, there is a little kid inside every one of us. Some are just a little better at hiding it than others."

I looked at my grandma and chuckled.

Then we met Mr. and Mrs. McGregor as we turned the corner. They lived right around the block from my grandma in a tiny white house with a picket fence.

"My brother and sister, Angus and Fiona, are coming for a visit," Mr. McGregor said. "I haven't seen them for twenty years. Imagine! It took an event like this to bring us together."

We said good-bye to them and walked past the beauty parlor. I peeked in the window. All the chairs were full of women and girls waiting to get their hair and nails ready for the Extravaganza. Mrs. Atken's dress shop next door was busy with people buying new dresses, hats and shoes.

When we got home, I called Mr. Malloy on the phone. Cordelia hadn't arrived yet. Her plane was delayed. I wondered if she would make it on time.

The Kaiser Wilhelm

Chapter Ten
The Kaiser Wilhelm

The night before the Extravaganza, both Grandma and I were so excited we couldn't sleep. We sat on the old porch swing in our pajamas, under a bright yellow moon and shimmering stars. There was a warm summer breeze and a sweet smell that came from the rose garden near the porch. I looked at the trellises filled with red, yellow and pink roses. We had worked so hard planting, digging, watering and trimming them over the years.

Grandma stared off into space.

"Are you thinking about the Extravaganza?" I asked.

"No, Julie. I'm thinking about the time I traveled on the *Kaiser Wilhelm.*"

"Tell me about it."

She put her arm gently around me. "I was thinking about how much the trip changed us."

"Changed you?"

"Yes. The long voyage changed us. You see, Julie, we came from small villages and had lived there most of our lives. Many of us lived inland and worked on farms or in factories and never even saw a ship, especially such a big one like the *Kaiser Wilhelm.*"

"Were you scared?"

"Yes we were scared. Late at night on the *Kaiser Wilhelm,* we could hear moaning from the howling winds. Stories spread that the sound was from the people who went down on the *Titanic* crying for help. I knew it wasn't true, because I didn't believe in ghosts. But still, Julie, it sent chills up and down my spine to hear the stories and moaning night after night."

"It gives me chills just to think about it, Grams."

"Some people just like to scare others. But we knew it was the seamen on the ship that started the stories, because most of us never even knew or heard about the *Titanic.* Our newspapers printed local events and news traveled slowly in those days."

"Tell me more."

"Well, we were crowded together on a ship with people we couldn't communicate with or even understand. We had a lot to learn. Sometimes our differences led to tempers running wild and fights breaking out on the ship."

"You mean fist fights?"

"Yes, some bad ones, too. Why, I still remember one fight when one older man with a beard saw a young man with his wife's blanket in his hand. He thought the man had stolen it. The young man tried to explain, but they couldn't understand each other's language."

"What did they do?"

"The man with the beard hauled off and punched the young man so hard he almost knocked him overboard. Then the young man got up and returned the blow. The fight didn't end until the older man's wife threw a bucket of water on him. She told her husband the young man's baby just died and she gave the man the blanket for his wife. Come to find out, the young man had wrapped his dead son in his own blanket before they lowered the child into the sea. The man with the beard felt so awful."

"Oh, Grams. That's sad."

"Yes, it was, Julie. But the story about that fight spread and others were not so quick to start trouble after that."

"Did everyone get along?"

"No, fear and superstitions caused misunderstandings and made people's lives so hard. Then to make it even worse, we were packed in like sardines with our stomachs turned upside down from the swaying of the ship. Why, there was no telling what would happen. It's a wonder we made it at all." She pushed her feet off the ground causing the swing to sway. "But we learned from our fear."

"You did?"

"Yes, Julie, we did. None of us felt the same when they walked the ramp to Ellis Island. We had to learn to get along. I remember that last night on the ship." She looked up at the sky. "The moon was big and full and the stars were shining their brightest, just like tonight. We could see the torch of the Statue of Liberty and lights from Ellis Island. It was a time for celebration."

"What did you do?'

"Families sat together gathering for a festive night. The Scots got out their bagpipes; the Irish their fiddles; the Germans their accordions; and everyone began a night of song and dance. They put aside their differences and had a friendly competition to see who could play the loudest and dance the longest."

"It must have been so much fun."

"Oh, it was. It was the greatest competition I'd ever seen." Grandma's eyes watered and glistened in the moonlight. "We were united that night in a special bond; survivors of our own fear and the many weeks of the long dangerous voyage over turbulent seas on the *Kaiser Wilhelm.* The next day, a new breed of people walked down the wooden plank with more understanding and more tolerance of what makes us all unique."

Both Grandma and I sat quietly for a while rocking on the porch swing.

I thought about tomorrow and the grand reunion of two friends who survived the trip together on the *Kaiser Wilhelm*.

Would Cordelia arrive on time?

A Surprise Meeting

Chapter Eleven

A Secret Meeting

"Grams. Can you believe it? Today is the day of the Extravaganza."

Grandma rolled out the cookie dough with her wooden rolling pin. I mixed the chopped walnuts, eggs, butter and honey. My mouth watered at the thought of eating nut-horn cookies made with cream cheese dough and walnut filling.

"Don't be drooling. They won't be done until you get back. You'd better get out of your pajamas. Mrs. Peterson will be picking you up soon to help her deliver the welcome baskets to the town's visitors."

I heard a car blow its horn in front of our house. In a flash I was dressed and on my way out the door.

"Hello, Mrs. Peterson," I said as I jumped in the front seat. "Can we stop by to see Mr. Malloy first? I'm worried about Cordelia. She was supposed to be here yesterday, but her plane was delayed."

"Sure, Julie. But let's deliver a couple of baskets on the way."

I turned to look in the back seat. It was filled with brightly colored baskets stuffed with fruit, candies and homemade cookies. They were wrapped in clear plastic and decorated with green and yellow ribbons.

"They sure are pretty. And they look yummy too," I said.

"They are lovely, aren't they? The Women's Club made them yesterday for some of our distinguished guests."

"Are you excited about the Extravaganza tonight?" I asked.

"I think everyone in town is."

"I sure am. I can't wait."

She turned down Usher Street and then made a left on Emory. "Where are we going?" I asked.

"The first stop is The Blakelee's Inn." She pulled in front of a big yellow house with white pillars and a veranda that went around the front and side. As we stepped inside, it felt like we had gone back into Victorian times. Everything was decorated with flowers, frills and lace.

"Julie, would you mind taking this basket upstairs to the second room on the right? I'd like to talk to Mrs. Blackelee for a few minutes."

I took the basket, hopped up the stairs and knocked on the second door to the right. A soft voice from inside said to come in. I opened the door and saw pink walls, pink curtains and rose-colored flowers that decorated pictures, bedspreads and carpets. The room had two single beds, a desk and a sitting area with two overstuffed high-backed chairs. A woman elegantly dressed in a light green dress with a delicate lace collar sat in one of the chairs. Her gray hair was braided on top of her head. She motioned for me to sit and offered me some tea.

After welcoming her to the town, I set the basket on the table next to her and said, "I'm sorry but I can't stay. I have to help Mrs. Peterson deliver some more welcome baskets."

"I'm sure she won't mind, Julie. Come sit a while." She patted the chair next to her.

"How do you know my name?" I asked as I sat down.

"You don't know who I am, do you? Why my dear Julie, I am Cordelia Grimm."

My mouth hung open and I stared into her blue eyes. Tiny curls fell about her face. Although delicate looking and thin, she had pink cheeks and smooth skin. My eyes widened as I leaned forward in the chair, speechless.

"I've heard a great deal about you, Julie, but no one told me you were shy—no, quite the contrary. An out-spoken, lively child is what I have been led to believe. Whatever could be the matter?"

Tears stung my eyes. "I didn't think you would make it in time or that I would ever get to meet you. Sometimes I would get so mad at myself for my dreaming and the anxiety it caused me. Just when I thought everything would work out so well and be so easy, I found myself in the middle of a lot of worrying. And then just when it seemed like my dream would never come true... well, here you are."

"Come." She stood up and pulled me up into her arms. Tears flowed freely, hers and mine. She took an embroidered hankie out of her pocket and dried my eyes. "My sweet little Julie, never stop dreaming. Why, your dream is the very reason I am here. You not only found the fairy tale, but you got Mr. Malloy to put it in the town's newspaper. When I first heard from *The Daily Covington Times,* I couldn't believe it. I had forgotten all about my dream to get the fairy tale published. Leave it to a grandchild of Anna's to remind us to keep a dream in our hearts and a fairy tale in our heads."

"The fairy tale. A part of it is missing. Did you finish translating it?"

"Yes I did. It was hard to translate and I did have trouble remembering the ending. But I think tonight when it's read, you'll be delighted."

"You're going to read it tonight at the Extravaganza?"

"Yes I am. And not only that, but Mr. Malloy is going to distribute tomorrow's newspaper tonight with the fairy tale inside."

"He is?" I gasped in delight.

"Yes, Julie, he is. Please have a seat. " She sat down and poured tea into a tiny cup, handed it to me and pointed to a silver tray with decorated cookies. "Come have some tea."

I sat down, took the cup and stirred three lumps of sugar into the tea. "Thank you for the tea, Cordelia. I'm afraid I'll have to pass on the cookies though. It's hard for me to swallow right now."

"Yes, I guess all this news at once must be quite a shock for you."

"It sure is but not as much as it will be for my grandma. She has been so exasperating this whole week. All she talks about is you and all the horrible things that could have happened to you on the way back to Germany. I had all I could do not to tell her you were coming. It's been the hardest secret I've ever had to keep."

Cordelia chuckled. "Soon, my dear, you won't have to hold it in any longer. Mr. Malloy and I will meet you at the Extravaganza and we'll work out the plans to surprise your grandma."

Mrs. Peterson came into the room. "Better go now so your grandma won't get suspicious."

I gave Cordelia a great big hug and then drifted down the stairs in a daze.

After we delivered the rest of the baskets, Mrs. Peterson brought me home.

The sweet smell of freshly baked nut-horns filled the house. Grandma came to meet me with a handful. She laughed. "I knew you couldn't wait. I'm sure that's all you thought about while you were delivering the welcome baskets."

All I thought about, if she only knew. I gobbled the nut-horns up, keeping my eyes on the cookies and avoiding eye contact with Grams. I was glad she was too busy trying to get everything ready for the Extravaganza to ask me any questions.

The secret was still safe.

Gazebo

Chapter Twelve
The Extravaganza Begins

It was time. I couldn't believe we were finally getting dressed for the Extravaganza. Grandma and I put on our new light-blue silk dresses trimmed with white lace and bows. Then we put on the shoes we had dyed light blue to match. My grandma put my hair up with little gold-butterfly clips and curled tiny ringlets around my face. I helped Grandma with her hair and slipped glittering combs around her French twist. When we finished getting ready, we held each other's hand, looked into the long mirror and grinned.

I felt so elegant as we walked to town arm-in-arm and greeted people along the way. When we crossed the street in town, I peeked into the firehouse recreation hall. I saw long rows of tables along the back wall set up with all kinds of food. There were glass vases with big clumps of pink and yellow carnations set up on the tables. The park, in the middle of town, was brightly decorated with blue, yellow and green lanterns hanging from trees and around the gazebo. Streamers were draped around trees and poles. Grandma said such a festive sight has not been seen in Covington for quite some time.

When Grandma got busy talking to her friends, I left her side and started searching for Cordelia and Mr. Malloy.

I walked into the firehouse and smelled the turkey, roast beef and corn on the cob. I drooled over the fried chicken and chocolate cake. I was attempting to grab a chicken leg when I felt a bony hand clamp onto my shoulder. I gasped, jumped back, spun around and saw Miss Eagle Eyes looking at me. Her eyes were the same eagle eyes, but her face wasn't all pinched up. She had on a flowing dress with purple flowers and she had a smile on her face.

"So there you are, Julie. Mr. Malloy and I have been looking for you," she said. Then a tall, thin man with dark rimmed glasses came over and put an arm around Miss Eagle Eye's shoulder. He asked her to dance and to my surprise, she said yes. I wondered who he could be. As they headed toward the front door, she turned and said to me, "Mr. Malloy and someone else are waiting for you out the back door." Then Miss Eagle Eyes winked at me.

I stared at them with my mouth hanging open. When I realized how silly I must look, I closed my mouth and hurried out the back door. Then I heard whispering sounds coming from around the corner. "Psst—psst, Julie?"

Cordelia and Mr. Malloy were standing under a tree. They motioned for me to come and join them. Mr. Malloy was dressed in a black tuxedo with a starched white shirt and a black bow tie. Cordelia looked like a queen with her long hair braided around her head with sparkling green jewels pinned in her hair. Her long empire-style, cream-colored dress was trimmed with the same pastel green as the jewels on her neck and in her hair.

"There you are," Mr. Malloy said as he took my arm.

"Does your grandma suspect anything?" Cordelia asked.

"No, nothing. She's convinced herself that you're dead." I said.

"Dead? That's awful! Poor, poor Anna." Cordelia put her hand over her mouth.

Mr. Malloy huddled us together and said, "Well, she'll soon find out you're not dead, won't she? Now listen to my plan. I will welcome the visitors and go through the usual speeches. I'll mention solving the mysteries related to the Brothers Grimm's lost fairy tale. Julie, that's when you'll join Cordelia in the back of the gazebo and wait for your names to be called. Don't worry about your grandma; I have someone to keep her busy."

Cordelia and I nodded our heads in agreement. Then Mr. Malloy walked away and left us alone.

I said to Cordelia, "You look so elegant—just like a queen. I love your dress and the green jewels. They're so beautiful."

"Why thank you, dear. You look very lovely and so grown up tonight." She twirled her index finger around one of my curls and smiled.

"It is fun to get dressed up and to see everyone looking so nice. Isn't it Cordelia?"

"It certainly does add to a festive atmosphere."

"And the food... I can smell it from here," I said. "I can't wait to eat. Can you?"

"I'm afraid I'm too nervous to eat anything right now."

A man and a woman walked close by. We heard them talking about the fairy tale. Cordelia and I stood quiet and listened to them.

"Do you suppose they'll release it tonight?" the woman asked the man.

"I don't know. But it's certainly the talk of the town," he answered.

"I can't wait until they tell us who found the fairy tale."

"I reckon since *The Daily Covington Times* is involved in the festivities tonight, they'll have some surprises," he said. "The article Mr. Malloy put in the newspaper has got the whole town stirred up. I'm sure he has a plan."

As they walked away, their voices drifted off.

"Everyone is talking about the fairy tale. Are you nervous, Cordelia, about reading in front of so many people?"

"I guess you could say I am. I didn't get much sleep last night and I couldn't eat a thing all day. But you don't need to worry about me. I'll be fine. You'd better go find your grandma or she'll be sending out a search party for you."

After giving her a hug, I headed for the food. The same chicken leg called out to me. As I reached to get it, I heard my grandma's voice.

"I thought I'd find you here," Grandma said. "Hurry, come with me. I think Mr. Malloy is about to give his speech."

She put one arm around me and we walked toward the front door. I looked back at all the food, wondering if I would ever get to eat any of it.

When we walked across the street to the park, the band started to play and the crowd swarmed toward the gazebo. My heart pounded. It was time.

What will my grandma do when she sees Cordelia?

The Mysterious Travel Chest

Chapter Thirteen
The Grand Surprise

We heard the drum-roll from the band playing in the immense gazebo set up in the corner of the park. Grandma and I looked to see what was happening. We saw Mr. Malloy walk up to the microphone. The band stopped playing and Mr. Malloy looked at the audience. He thanked the businesses for their kind donations and all the people who had worked so hard to make the Extravaganza possible. He also welcomed friends, family and visitors to the town of Covington. Then two men carried Cordelia's travel chest that I had found in the attic and set it in front of the microphone.

"I suppose you are wondering about the unsolved mystery involving the lost fairy tale found in this travel chest," he said as he pointed to the chest. "Who found it? Who translated it? And when it will be published?"

Mrs. Peterson came over, tugged at my grandma's arm and began to whisper to her. When my grandma turned to listen, Mrs. Peterson gave me a wink. I headed towards the back of the gazebo. I joined Cordelia and held her hand as we waited for Mr. Malloy to call our names.

"The mysteries involving this old travel chest have been a well-kept secret," Mr. Malloy said, "and you needn't wonder any longer." He called my grandma to come up on the gazebo.

Mr. Malloy walked over to the steps, took my grandma's hand and escorted her to the microphone. She stood next to him as he continued his speech. He explained about the *Kaiser Wilhelm*, the ship Grandma and Cordelia had traveled together on so long ago. He told the audience that they had my grandma to thank for this festive night because of a promise she kept to her friend, Cordelia Grimm. He explained that she had kept the treasured travel chest safe for more than fifty years and that was where both the letter and the lost fairy tale were found.

Cordelia and I took deep breaths and squeezed each other's hands tight as we listened to the applause.

"Ahh... but the travel chest was forgotten," Mr. Malloy said, "until someone climbed the old attic stairs and was drawn to open this very travel chest." He pointed to the travel chest in front of him again. "Would you like to meet this person?" He turned toward the back of the gazebo, called my name and motioned for me to join them.

My knees felt weak as I climbed the stairs. I hurried over to Grandma and grabbed her hand. I looked out at the audience and they looked like shadowy figures in the distance. Mr. Malloy's voice sounded muffled as he explained how I had found the fairy tale and asked him to publish it in the *Daily Covington Times*. My heart beat hard and fast as I listened to the crowd's applause. I moved closer to Grandma and squeezed her hand.

"Now for the mystery question of who translated the fairy tale," Mr. Malloy said. "We wanted to have as accurate a translation as possible, so we contacted someone from Germany to do the translating. Tonight this translator is our most honored guest and has traveled a great distance to be with us. She is the great, great granddaughter of one of the Brothers Grimm. May I present, Cordelia Grimm."

My grandma's eyes glistened with tears and her mouth dropped open as she watched Cordelia walk toward her. "I can't believe it. Oh my! Is it really you?"

"Yes, my dear Anna, it is," Cordelia said.

The audience was silent as they watched the two friends wrap their arms tightly around each other. Tears flowed from Cordelia, Grandma, the onlookers and me.

"But that's not all," Mr. Malloy said. "There's one more surprise."

The tall man with the dark-rimmed glasses who had asked Miss Eagle Eyes to dance appeared.

"This is Mr. Haverson from Colbier Press," Mr. Malloy said. "He's an old friend of Miss Cragmyer. She contacted him to see if his company would consider publishing the fairy tale. He has agreed to publish it in a Grimm's Fairy Tale picture book for children."

I couldn't believe what I was hearing. The story of Princess Momalina and Katrianna Jonatina Breosio published in a picture book! I jumped and kicked my feet in the air.

We were surrounded by thundering applause.

Mr. Malloy put his hands up and quieted the crowd. Grandma and I were escorted to our seats in the front row. We sat down and held on to each other. "Would you like to hear Cordelia read the fairy tale?" Mr. Malloy asked.

Then after all the hoots, hollers and loud clapping was silenced, Mr. Malloy held out his hand and invited Cordelia to the microphone to read the lost fairy tale.

Katrianna's Village Home

Chapter Fourteen
The Lost Fairy Tale

Cordelia stood gracefully with her head held high. Her face looked radiant as she looked around at the audience. The green jewels on her neck and in her hair glittered. Mr. Malloy handed Cordelia a copy of the fairy tale. If a full moon could smile, I think it did at that very moment.

There was silence.

Cordelia announced the name of the fairy tale, *Princess Momalina.* Then she began to read the fairy tale in a powerful storyteller's voice.

Once upon a long time ago, nestled between a dark forest and a white-tipped mountain was a tiny village. Blue, yellow and purple pansies popped out of the window boxes of the small, whitewashed stone houses in the village square.

In one of the houses lived a little girl named Katrianna Jonatina Breosio. She had golden hair, bright blue eyes and the prettiest dresses in the village. Her father, Popa, worked in a cloth mill and her mother, Moma, sewed at home for some of the village folk. There was always enough material left over to make beautiful clothes for Katrianna.

One day, Moma and Popa decided to surprise Katrianna with a new doll. Moma took great care picking out just the right pieces from the cloth Popa brought home from the mill. She stuffed the little doll with the softest cotton and sewed on glittery deep-blue buttons for eyes. With red silk thread, she sewed on a smile and then used black thread to make a tiny nose and curly eyelashes. She embroidered a little pink heart on the doll's chest with a yellow flower around it. Then she sewed long locks of golden yarn to the doll's head, twisted them into braids and tied yellow silk ribbons on the ends.

From the red, yellow and green pieces of cloth, Moma made dresses, bonnets and jackets to match. She even sewed some pajamas.

After that, she took the soft yellow silk cloth and made a fancy party dress. She embroidered pansies around the edges and even embroidered some on the cloak, hat and slippers. She sewed a small yellow bag to keep the fancy party dress neat and clean.

When Katrianna saw the doll, she fell in love with it at once.

"Oh, Moma," she said. "She's beautiful! I shall name her Princess Momalina after you."

Everyday Katrianna changed the doll's clothes and took her everywhere she went. She only took out the yellow silk dress on very special occasions.

The people who lived in the village worked hard all day and in the evening gathered in the village square. They sang songs and danced to the lively music of accordions, tambourines and fiddles.

Moma and Popa took Katrianna and Princess Momalina to dance and sing songs with the village folk.

The people were happy because a good king ruled over the little village between the dark forest and the white-tipped mountain. But not all kings were good.

When the people from the dark-forest heard the music from the little village, they became jealous. They complained to the king of the dark forest that the singing of the village people was mocking the dark forest king. The king was angry and one day he came out of the dark forest and chased the good king and all the people from the village.

Moma, Popa and Katrianna had to flee in the middle of the night.

Popa carried blankets, warm clothing and tools that they would need for their journey. Moma carried food, pots and pans. Katrianna carried shoes and some of her clothes in a burlap sack. She stuffed the yellow-silk bag with the doll's party dress deep inside it. Then she tucked Princess Momalina on top of the burlap sack and tied the string around the sack with the doll's head sticking out.

They ran toward the white-tipped mountain away from the dark forest and the bad king. Behind them, they heard the sound of pounding hooves of horses and voices of men shouting.

Popa grabbed Moma and Katrianna and hid under bushes until the men and horses went by. Princess Momalina fell out of the bag when Popa pulled Moma and Katrianna out of the bushes and ran up the mountainside. They didn't know the doll was missing until it was too late.

Katrianna stood on the mountainside and looked down at the valley below. She would miss her little village home and her beautiful doll.

"Don't worry so about Princess Momalina," Popa said as he put his arm around Katrianna. "She is a beautiful

doll and was made with much love. One day she will be found by someone who will love her as much as you do."

Cordelia stopped reading and said, "This is all that could be translated from the fairy tale found in the travel chest. Due to the age of the manuscript much of the print was faded and the conclusion of the story was quite unreadable."

I heard people sighing and whispering in the audience. Grandma looked at me with her brows pinched together. She said, "It's a sad way to end a story."

I heard a man behind me say, "I thought Mr. Haverson was going to publish the fairy tale into a picture book for children. He certainly can't do it with that ending, can he?"

I bit my lower lip and looked up at Cordelia. I wanted to go to her and hold her hand. Then I remembered her telling me I would be delighted with the ending.

"There is more," I whispered.

I kept my eye on Cordelia.

Keep a dream
in your heart
and a fairy tale
in your head.

Chapter Fifteen
Beautiful Dreamer

Cordelia stepped aside when Mr. Malloy walked up to the microphone.

"I'd say that's not the way to end a fairy tale, is it?" he said. He looked around at the crowd as he twisted his mustache with one hand. Many in the audience mumbled and grumbled as they whispered to each other.

I poked my grandma's arm with my elbow. "There has to be more."

Mr. Malloy straightened his bow tie, pulled out some papers from his jacket and set them on the podium as two men took the travel chest away.

Slowly silence spread.

"Cordelia and I both agreed we needed to find the ending to the fairy tale," he said. "But recollections of the story's ending were somewhat vague to Cordelia, as she was only a child when she read it. She had to invent some of the fairy tale herself. When you hear the ending, I think you will agree with me that Cordelia has inherited a great deal of creative talent from the Grimm family. Would you like to hear what she wrote?"

The crowd applauded so loud that it hurt my ears. Grandma put her arm around me, smiled and gave me a hopeful glance.

Cordelia returned to the microphone, picked up the papers from the podium and waited. When there was silence, she looked down at the manuscript and began to read.

Many years passed. Katrianna grew up and had a little girl of her own. When she saw her little girl, she fell in love with her at once. She named her Tarastasha; but they called her Tara. She never told her little girl about her doll, Princess Momalina. It was just too sad.

One day, Katrianna got a letter from her old village. It said there was a new king in the land and her stone house was being returned to her. She was to come to the village and claim her house.

Katrianna took Tara to travel with her to her old village home. As they walked through the village, Tara stopped and pointed to a doll with a frilly bonnet in the window of a small antique store.

"Look, Mama! She is so beautiful and I love her."

Tara tugged on her mother and begged her to go inside.

Katrianna told the woman behind the counter she wanted to buy the doll in the window for her little girl.

The woman got the doll and handed it to Tara.

"I made the bonnet and dress myself," the woman said. "I just put the doll in the window today. My husband found it long ago hidden under bushes just outside the village. I've kept it wrapped in a special box until I could open this shop."

After paying for the doll, they took her home.

Katrianna saw how much Tara loved the doll and decided to make her new clothes. She told Tara to bring her the doll. When Katrianna looked at the blue button eyes and the faded red silk smile, she thought of Princess Momalina. As she took off the dress, she saw a tiny pink heart embroidered inside a yellow flower.

"Oh, my little Princess Momalina," she cried as she held the doll close to her heart. "It is you!"

Katrianna ran up the stairs and came back with a small shoebox. She sat down with Tara and told her the story about Princess Momalina. When she finished, she handed her daughter the shoebox and told her to open it. Inside, Tara saw the yellow silk bag Moma had made. When she untied the string to the bag, she found the beautiful yellow silk dress with pansies embroidered all around the edges, the cape, hat and slippers to match. They fit Princess Momalina just right.

"Oh, Mama." Tara said. "She is the most beautiful doll there ever was."

Katrianna Jonatina Breosio held Princess Momalina with outstretched arms and twirled her around the room.

And she saw the doll's blue button eyes twinkle.

When Cordelia finished reading, the crowd got up from their seats with resounding applause. She backed away from the microphone and bowed. Grandma and I stood and clapped our hands above our heads. I saw tears roll down my grandma's face and felt tears run down mine.

Mr. Malloy's face beamed as he walked over and put his arm around Cordelia. Miss Eagle Eyes bounded up the stairs to the gazebo carrying a huge bouquet of yellow, long stemmed roses. She handed them to Cordelia as Mr. Haverson walked up and stood by her side.

I heard Mrs. Peterson behind me tell someone that Mr. Malloy was right. Cordelia Grimm certainly has inherited a great deal of talent from the Brothers Grimm. Why, you couldn't even tell the difference in the style of the fairy tale's ending from its beginning.

I felt goose bumps pop up all over me.

Mr. Malloy motioned for the band to start playing and for Grandma and me to come up on the gazebo. When we got to the top of the steps Mr. Malloy took my grandma's hand. Mr. Haverson and Miss Eagle Eyes stood next to them.

The band was playing the song "Beautiful Dreamer." Cordelia pulled me to the middle of the gazebo. Grandma, Mr. Malloy, Miss Eagle Eyes and Mr. Haverson stood off to the side and smiled as they watched us.

Cordelia closed her eyes and swayed softly to the music. After a while, she opened her eyes and looked deep into my mine. Her lips said the words "beautiful dreamer, how I love you."

With outstretched arms and our hands clasped together, we twirled round and round.

Then, for a moment in time, I was Katrianna Jonatina Breosio.

And I saw Cordelia's blue eyes twinkle.

About the Author

Janie Lancaster grew up in Middletown, New York. She has two grown children and a teenage granddaughter. She now lives in southern California with her husband Don, her blue-eyed childhood sweetheart. After working as a sign language interpreter for the last fifteen years and a college professor for seven, she has set out on a course to fulfill her childhood dream to publish her written works.

The 1997 Wildacres Children's Book Writers Workshop in North Carolina picked Janie as "the most determined to be a writer." She has gone to numerous conferences sponsored by The Society of Children's Book Writers & Illustrators, The San Diego Book Awards Association, and The San Diego Writers/Editors Guild. She has written three children's novels, fifteen picture books and numerous poems. At the time of this writing, she is in the process of editing and getting her books ready for publication.

Her first novel, ***Julie & The Lost Fairy Tale***, is being printed as a serial story in newspapers across the country, through the Newspapers in Education programs where children read newspapers in classrooms.

More stories to come and free teacher's lesson plans for this book on line.

Visit Janie Lancaster online at:
http://www.janielancaster.com/

Note from the Author

My Dear Readers,

I hope you enjoyed my story *Julie & the Lost Fairy Tale.* This story was a fulfillment of my childhood dream to live with my grandma in a small town and do something wonderful.

To write my story, I became a time traveler. I traveled back and forth through time by reading books in libraries, looking through old picture albums at home, remembering and gathering bits and pieces of information that would be woven into my story of Julie.

Many people helped me get my story ready for publishing by reading it and giving me advice along the way. And I'll tell you a secret. I also use spell check on my computer because I can't spell.

My grandma really did come from Austria to Ellis Island on the Kaiser Wilhelm in 1913. Even though she died when I was only six years old, I've always remembered her loving kindness to me.

When I grew up, I walked through Covington, Georgia, with its small town charm and tree lined streets and dreamt about what it would have been like to grow up there with my grandma.

After I wrote my story of Julie, I flew to Covington, Georgia, and met David Rigas, the Editor of *The Covington News* and asked him to publish my story in his newspaper. I wanted to make my little girl dream come true.

David Rigas agreed to print my story and then he told me about Newspapers In Education where children read newspapers in classrooms. I printed my story in newspapers around the country and even in St Johns, Canada.

Never give up on your dreams, even if you have to wait for a very long time. You see, dreams really do come true.

Sincerely,
Janie Lancaster

References

http://www.ellisisland.org

Our Yesterdays—
A Pictorial History of Newton County, Georgia
The Covington News
Published by D-books Publishing Inc.

Main Street Covington
From its Creation to Modern Times
Peggy Lamberson
Printed by Thomson-Shore Inc.

Printed in the United States
64189LVS00004B/67-111

9 781932 993608